Pirate House Swap

Abie Longstaff

illustrated by Mark Chambers

PICTURE CORGI

Every year the Clark family spent the summer at home in the city. Mr Clark put up shelves and watched sport on the telly.

Mrs Clark repainted the lounge.

Emily played in the garden,

and Justin tried to join in.

But this summer they wanted to do something different.
They just didn't know what, until Mr Clark found
an advert with the perfect answer –
a house swap!

There were so many different houses to choose from.
But nothing seemed quite right . . .
until they turned the page and saw:

CLASSIFIED

Holidays

Grizzly Cottage

Too hot? Too cold?
Grizzly Cottage is
just right.
Sleeps 3,
porridge included.

Gingerbread Cottage

Deliciously rendered
Children welcome

Macdonald's Farm

An oink-oink here,
a quack-quack there,
the best little getaway anywhere!

Beautiful Castle

In sleepy town
Dense thicket hedge
Princes only

Holiday Home Swap

Lovely timber home.
Picturesque views.
Right on the sea – fish, swim and sail!
Sleeps four.

CLASSIFIED

Personal Ads

Feeling like an
ugly sister?
Visit THE FAIRYTALE
HAIRDRESSER and
live happily ever after.
Special introductory
offer: seven dwarfs for
the price of six!

Would like to meet
my queen of the
ocean. I'll be your
king. I have GSOH,
patch on one eye,
one wooden leg.

Looking for
lovely lady to
share cosy nights
under the stars.
Must like boats!

FOUND:
One slipper, size six,
glass. Contact P.
Charming, Box 263.

FOR SALE:
magic beans.
Not for eating.
May cause giants.
One cow o.n.o.
Box 320

It was perfect. Emily and Justin loved the seaside, Mrs Clark liked swimming and Mr Clark had visions of catching a fish "this big!".

HOW to...
Catch
BiG
FiSh

Their letters arrived
the very next day.

Subject: House Swap
From: The Clarks <theclarks@rbooks.com>
To: yepyrates@arrjimlad.com

We saw your details and would
love to swap houses next week.
We live in a little house on the
edge of the city.

(directions attached)

buy
new
eye-patch

Aaaarr! Your house sounds just
right, land lubbers.

With a fair wind we will be there
on the 15th.

Directions in the post,
ye savvy?

Grog

bucket
+
spade

suncream
sunglasses
Hat!

So the following week the Clarks left the key under the mat and set off for the coast.

At the harbour they followed the map.

Ye Olde pier

City

Dangerous Shoals

shark cove

whirlpool of Doom

They couldn't wait

to see their holiday home . . .

. . . but when they got there it **wasn't quite** what they were expecting!

The first day was hard work.

Mrs Clark accidentally fired the cannons

Mr Clark dropped his glasses overboard

Emily fell out of her hammock.

And Justin forgot to feed Silver, the parrot.

But every day was easier and easier and before long they began to feel totally at home.

Mrs Clark could hoist the mainsail in three seconds flat.

Emily mastered navigating by the stars.

Meanwhile at the
Clarks' house . . .

All too soon it was
time to go.

The Clarks said goodbye
to Silver and rowed back
to the old pier.

They were sad that they had to
leave so soon – it had been the
best holiday **ever!**

But when they arrived home . . .

. . . they found their house swap guests
had made a few changes.

The neighbours were not best pleased either.

Mr Peters' son
had a tattoo.

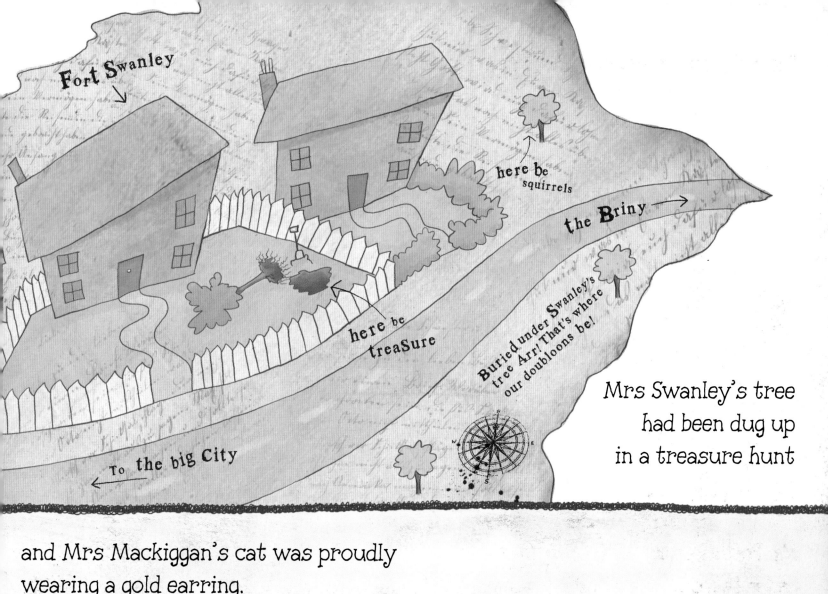

Fort Swanley

here be
squirrels

the Briny →

here be
treaSure

Buried under Swanley's
tree Arr! That's where
our doubloons be!

To the big City

Mrs Swanley's tree
had been dug up
in a treasure hunt

and Mrs Mackiggan's cat was proudly
wearing a gold earring.

The Clarks set about putting everything right. Mr Clark cleaned the house.

Mrs Clark washed off little Jimmy Peters' tattoo, (it was only felt tip)

and Emily and Justin replanted Mrs Swanley's tree.

But no one could get the earring off the cat as he liked it too much, so Mrs Clark gave Mrs Mackiggan some flowers.

By nightfall, everything was back to normal.
Mr Clark put the soup on, Emily set
the table, and Justin got the bread.

And Mrs Clark?

Well – she didn't do anything.
She was too busy looking at the
newspaper and trying to decide
who to swap with next year.